Library of Congress Cataloging-in-Publication Data:
Katz, Bobbi. Poems for small friends / by Bobbi Katz ; illustrated by Gyo Fujikawa.   p.   cm. SUMMARY: A collection of poems, including "Berry Picking," "The Truth
About Dogs," "Conversation with a Kite," and "My Travel Tree." ISBN: 0-394-81945-4 (trade) ; 0-394-91945-9 (lib. bdg.) 1. Children's poetry, American.
[1. American poetry] I. Fujikawa, Gyo, ill. II. Title   PS3561.A7518P6   1989   811'.54 – dc19   88-27444
Manufactured in the United States of America   1 2 3 4 5 6 7 8 9 0

POEMS

for
Small Friends

Poems by
BOBBI KATZ

•

Pictures by
GYO FUJIKAWA

RANDOM HOUSE 🏠 NEW YORK

MORNING SONG

Today is a day to catch tadpoles.
Today is a day to explore.
Today is a day to get started.
Come on! Let's not sleep anymore.

Outside the sunbeams are dancing.
The leaves sing a rustling song.
Today is a day for adventures,
and I hope that you'll come along!

FREE TO GOOD HOMES

Kittens today!
Kittens today!
If you promise to love them,
I'll give them away!

Ready to cuddle.
Ready to play.
Soft, purry kittens—
I'll give them away.

BERRY PICKING

Strawberries,
      strawberries—
yum, yum, yummy!
One for the pail
      and
two for the tummy!

One to save
      and
two to taste—
lots to pick
      and
none to waste!

The Truth About Dogs

Dogs want to be best friends with you.
   They understand things. Yes, they do.
"Sit, dog." "Stay, dog." "Here's a treat."
   Dogs are buddies. Dogs are sweet.
They wag their tails when they are glad.
   They seem to know when you are sad.

But running bunnies, squirrels, and cats
   drive any dog completely bats!
And anything you do or say
   won't make it "sit" or make it "stay."

THE DARE

I did it! I did it!
Now what about you?
You're stalling! You're stalling!
Come over here too!
Ready, set, go…
and JUMP
if you dare!

Stay there, scaredy-cats!
I don't care.

DRESS-UP

A treasure chest of castoff clothes!
    What's more fun, do you suppose?
With dandy costumes such as these
    we can dress up as we please!
A tie, a hat, a string of beads—
    are just the things that each kid needs!
Be a hunter or an elf—
    be *anyone*...except yourself!

Conversation with a Kite

Come back, come back, my runaway kite!
Come back and play with me!

I'm riding and gliding on whirl-away winds.
I'm going somewhere. Can't you see?

Where are you going, my beautiful kite,
flying so high in the sky?

I'm going to visit the lost balloons
that made little children cry.

When I held your string, oh my magical kite,
why did I feel the wind in my hand?

The wind is a taste of the sky, my young friend,
that I gave to a child of the land.

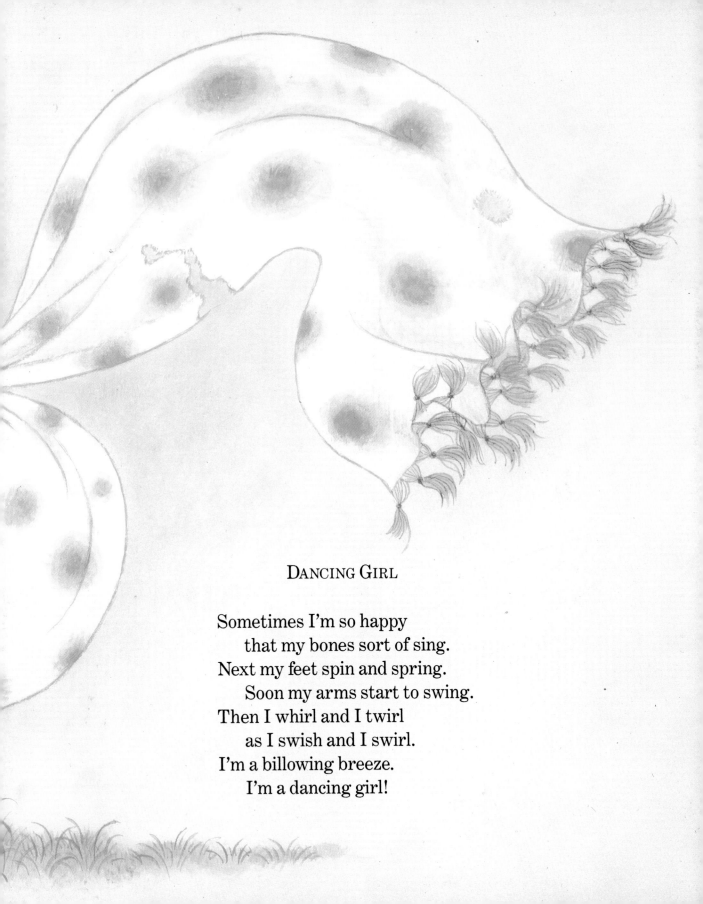

DANCING GIRL

Sometimes I'm so happy
    that my bones sort of sing.
Next my feet spin and spring.
    Soon my arms start to swing.
Then I whirl and I twirl
    as I swish and I swirl.
I'm a billowing breeze.
    I'm a dancing girl!

A WINTER THOUGHT

These three things belong together:
    kids and hills and snowy weather.
What a waste to have just snow
    without a hill where it can go!
Imagine a snow-covered hill
    without a single child to thrill!
Would grownups rush to get their sleds,
    or just complain and shake their heads?
Snow speaks to kids. They hear it say,
    "Make some snowballs! Come! Let's play!"

My Travel Tree

There are oh-so-many
kinds of trees—
apple, pear, pine—
but there is just one special tree
I feel is somehow mine.
Its branches form
such cozy nooks
for dreaming dreams
and reading books.
I sail to almost anywhere,
perched among the leaves up there.
If naming things were up to me,
I'd call this one my travel tree.

LEAVING HOME

I'm moving into your house.
I'm bringing my best stuff.
My parents have a baby —
they don't love me enough.
I think I am much nicer
than some baby in a bib
who has to wear a diaper
and sleep in some dumb crib.

Let them keep their baby
and listen to it bawl.
I'm moving into your house.
I don't need them at all!

GOOD-NIGHT SONG

Good night, little sleepyhead.
Snuggle in your cozy bed.
Tomorrow is another day
with friends to see and games to play.
Let the wind stay up all night!
But as for you—
sweet dreams. Sleep tight!